THE SECRET TO THE TREASURE OF
Rennes-le-Chateau

MICHAEL ALAN KUHN

Balboa Press books may be ordered through booksellers or by contacting:

Balboa Press
A Division of Hay House
1663 Liberty Drive
Bloomington, IN 47403
www.balboapress.com
1 (877) 407-4847

ISBN: 978-1-5043-9417-8 (sc)
ISBN: 978-1-5043-9418-5 (e)

Library of Congress Control Number: 2017918987

Print information available on the last page.

Balboa Press rev. date: 12/14/2017

BALBOA
PRESS
A DIVISION OF HAY HOUSE

DEDICATION

This book has no dedication as it comes from my heart. It has taken me a long time to let go of the limitation of what I was taught or learned to believe. It has taken me a long time to journey inward and follow my heart.

I ask you read with an open mind and heart.

For those that will criticize what I have presented in this book I would only ask, what if maybe?

THE SECRET TO THE TREASURE OF RENNES-le-CHATEAU

CHAPTERS

NOT WHAT YOU EXPECT

*I*t is always amazes me how the most wonderful adventures start in the simplest of ways. I do not know about you but I have had a tendency to always look for a reason or purpose to any journey or adventure in life. This time I would soon find out it was not what I expected. It was the beginning of a dramatic change through self-discovery to my perspective about what I have been taught or learned.

It is a beautiful spring day where the air is cool but you feel the warmth of the sun on your skin. I began my morning walk and all is quiet as very few people have begun to stir as it is the start of a leisurely weekend day. The sky is a light blue decorated with big fluffy white clouds and I am enjoying the birds singing greeting the beginning of the day.

I decide to stop at my mail box. I insert the key into the mail box and as I open the door I see a pink envelop with beautiful decorations of flowers and fairies. It could only be from one person, my dear friend Kathryn. She is a petite woman, green eyes, and very curly sandy brown hair flowing all the way down her back. She has the intensity of a charging bull, yet at the same time, the gentleness of an angel. Yes, a contradiction, but understandable of a person that is has chosen of life of a spiritual teacher.

I quickly opened the pink envelop and took out its contents. I unfolded the page and on the top of the page it was entitled "Path of the Divine Feminine." My mind quickly wonders why she would be inviting me. I am very much a male. Kathryn every two years presents spiritual quests to various parts of the world. She has taken groups to South Africa, Egypt, Greece, and many other wonderful places. This flyer is announcing her next excursion to the South of France to trace the journey in Mary Magdalene to Gaul (now France) after the death of Jesus. In the South of France there are many churches dedicated to Mary Magdalene and the Marys' who made the journey with her.

I wonder why Kathryn had sent me the flyer. It appeared to be a journey specifically for women. I place the flyer on my desk and soon forgot about it. A few weeks went by and Kathryn called me to ask if I had received the flyer. I told her I had received it. I expressed my impression that it was a journey primarily for women and not men. She quickly advised me that is was for all people. I told her I would think about it.

The following week I was watching the History Channel and the topic was about Rennes-le-Chateau in the south of France. The main theme was about speculation that the treasures of the Knight Templar had been discovered there. The program describe the very old little church that was there that had undergone restoration and the construction of new buildings. This is a farming community without the means to pay for such significant improvements. There was and has been speculation as to how the local priest was able to pay for all the improvements. Thus the speculation he had discovered hidden treasures. The story was fascinating and peaked my interest to maybe visit there.

Another few weeks had gone by and I had not thought about Kathryn's flyer about the excursion to the South of France. Now my cell phone is ringing and I can see that it is Kathryn calling. Without saying hello Kathryn asks if I am going on the journey as the deadline to commit to the trip was approaching. I again express my thoughts that this felt like it was a trip designed for women. Kathryn insisted it was for all people. I again told her I would think about it.

A few days go by and Kathryn is again calling. She again asks if I was going to go. I asked her why she was so insistent that I go. She laughed and said, "Well to be honest, most of the trip is by passenger vans she is renting and two of the people on the excursion will have to drive." I too laughed and asked, "So you need a driver?" She responded, "Yes." I laughed from deep inside me and said, "You should had said so the first time we talked. Yes, I will go and be a driver."

I sent off my check to pay for the excursion. In a few days I received the itinerary and began to read. I got excited especially when I saw that we would be spending a few days in Rennes-le-Chateau. A chance to see in person what I had seen on the History Channel. Wow, it must be destiny.

As it turns out, the group set for the journey was comprised of sixteen women and three men. The group was from all different regions of the United States and a few women from other parts of the world. All age groups were represented. At the end of summer our launching point for our adventure of the Path of the Divine Feminine was Marseille, France near the Italian border.

JOURNEY BEGINS

*I*n September 2011, we landed in Marseille ready to begin our journey of the path of the divine feminine in France's romantic south with it rolling hills and lush farmlands. The group's purpose for the journey was to visit the places Mary Magdalene visited and touched after she left Israel. In this region of the south of France you will find many churches dedicated to Mary Magdalene. Of particular interest are the many churches and holy sites dedicated to the Black Madonna. What does this mean? This stirred the intrigue for the adventure we were embarking upon.

I decided to go on this journey to support my friends on their spiritual quest and to have fun. Little did I know what was about to unfold in a small village in the middle of the picturesque rural south of France countryside.

Our adventures first took us to Marseille to visit the Saint Maxiumin-La-Sainte-Baume to visit the Basilica of Mary Magdalene which housed her relic – skull encased in gold.

Next our journeys took us to the Hotellerie de la Sainte-Baume. The Dominicans are the keepers of The Holy Cave – La Santé Baume) which is situated hundreds of feet up in the hillside cliffs. In the valley sits a church adjacent to the Monastery are various paintings of Mary Magdalene as she arrived in Gaul (France) and her travels through the south of France. What I found interesting is that the murals on the church walls depicted Mary Magdalene with radiant red hair.

The painting first catch your eye but soon your attention is drawn to the altar. There is a statue of Mary Magdalene holding a baby to the left of the altar. It was never said or discussed in the Monastery but some believe this statue depicts Mary Magdalene with her daughter Sarah from her union with Jesus. It is believed this may have been one of the inspiration for the theme in Dan Brown's book the Da Vinci Code.

Our journeys next took us to Arles. There I relaxed with my fellow male friends Albert and Lanny. Albert is a man of the world. He is hefty Hispanic man which fits as he was a campus supervisor before he retired. He is distinguished looking and his physical appearance does not give away his age. Everywhere we go people think he is native to the land. (We have yet to go to northern European countries to see if this still holds true.) Lanny is a semi-retired college professor whose doctorate is in History. He has a full head of curly gray hair – head and face. If you walk into any restaurant you would immediately be able to tell which man was the college professor. With both Albert and Lanny you gravitate to them and just want to sit and talk to them for hours. The three of us went to the main street, enjoying a beer, and watching the people of Arles as they go about their day.

On the fifth day we arrived in the romantic small village of Rennes-le-Chateau. The primary draw to this quaint village is the petite Church of Mary Magdalene situated at the dome of the hill with the village just below. The village overlooks, in all directions, the valley farmlands. Beyond the farmlands are small mountains that stand as if they are protecting this simple yet beautiful village and valleys. There are very few trees in the village or the surrounding areas. As you scan the panorama you have the feeling you are looking at painting, by one of the great masters, coming to life.

RENNES-le-CHATEAU

The village sits along a ridge and the top of a fifteen hundred foot hill overlooking the surrounding countryside and the twin villages of Couiza and Montazels. It has a colorful history including the Romans, Visigoths, Knights Templar, and Cathars. The village is hidden from valley below. The rolling hills are filled with farmlands and vineyards. The breath-taking views from the top of the hill reveal its command of the surrounding area. The buildings of the village line the only road leading up to the church and adjacent buildings. The buildings are primary stone facades and look as if they have not been touched in hundreds of years even though it has been rebuilt many times over the centuries. It is a small village with only about 100 inhabitants.

The church of Mary Magdalene sits at the top of the hill at the end of the village. Next to the church is a museum providing information about the Father Sauniere, the priest who oversaw the renovation of the church. The museum includes artifacts and history of the churches renovation from 1887 to 1897. These major renovations fueled the speculation about the source of the funds Father Sauniere used to renovate the church.

A portion of the museum is dedicated to Marie Denarnaud who was Father Sauniere's housekeeper and close confidante. She was born in 1868 and was twenty four years old when she arrived in Rennes-le-Chateau. Marie Denarnaud never revealed anything about the priest's secret. After Father Sauniere's death she told people that there is more wealth buried there that could support the town for more than one hundred years. Her comments fueling the speculation of buried treasures.

Father Sauiere arrived in Rennes-le-Chateau in June 1885 at the age of 33 and six years after being ordained. He is a big man with strong features and looks as if he spent his entire life working the fields or in the mills instead of in service to the church.

The village is internationally known for being the center of various treasurer and conspiracy theories. Legend has it that the impoverished parish priest, Berenger Sauniere, after arriving in 1885 began renovating the church in 1891 after it said he found mysterious documents. Some theories say he took these documents to Paris which brought him great fortune. With this great fortune he begins to renovate the church, dedicated to Mary Magdalene, with mysterious décor that many believe is a secret encoded for only those with eyes that can see.

Interestingly one of the new features is an inscription above the front door, which reads: "This is a place of awe; this is God's house, the gate of heaven, and it shall be called the royal court of God."

Sauniere also funded the construction of another structure at top of the hill adjacent to the church, also dedicated to Mary Magdalene, which he had stated was intended for retired priest.

With all the rumors and speculation about how Father Sauniere funded the church's restoration he was called to the Bishop of Carcassonne, Monseigneur Monsignor Felix Arsene Billard who oversaw his parish. The Bishop asked him how much he had spent on the renovation. He also inquired about the source of the funds that he used to renovate the church. Father Sauniere stated that he had spent over 193,000 francs.

Father Sauniere was put on trial in 1910 where he stated he raised the funds for the renovation by selling of masses. He died in 1917 in disgrace and impoverished.

THE CHURCH OF MARY MAGDALENE

T he Church of Mary Magdalene is about thirty feet wide and one hundred twenty feet in length. Your eye is drawn to the vivid colors, it's uniquely structure, and simple beauty. The altar gives you the impression of a house with each level built on a strong foundation, for what is above, as it reaches into the sky. The vivid colors of the altar are yellows, golds, and blues on a cream color background. However, what catches your eye is the wall behind and above the altar. As your eyes move upward, following the form of the altar, you cannot help but notice the royal blue ceiling with dozens of five-pointed golden stars. On a pedestals about eight feet above the floor, on the wall to the right of the altar, is a statue of Mother Mary holding the baby Jesus. The pedestal visually appears to be at the same height as the top tier of the altar. On the opposite wall, to the left of the altar, is another pedestal with a statue of Joseph also holding the baby Jesus. Very seldom do you see in churches or painting Joseph depicted holding the baby Jesus.

The altar is built in four distinct tiers. The base of the altar is about eight feet across and in the center of the base is a painting of Mary Magdalene looking up as if she is looking to heaven. There are many distinctive symbols in the painting that have religious and historians debating their meaning. Very seldom do you see Mary Magdalene depicted as the foundation or on the base of an altar.

The second tier of the altar is about three feet high and is the same height as the base. The second tier has two levels to its depth. The background is plain as to not distract from the meaning of the front. In the center of the second tier is a house like structure that is about eighteen inches wide and about thirty inches high. In the center of the rendering is a cup of that appears to depict the Holy Grail with two small figurines below and on either side. On the either side of the rendering are two pillars which appear to be the base supporting the structure above.

Resting on the two pillars is what appears to be a pitched roof much like what you would see in rural churches in the United States. On each side of this center structure of the second tier of the altar are three steps leading to the base of the pitched roof structure. There appears to be no purpose to these steps other than the pedestals to hold the tall candle sticks place their by the church.

The third tier of the altar sitting above the pitched roof structure of the second tier rises a flat platform supporting the very unique structure above. Rising from this flat platform are four ornate pillars supporting above another pitched roof structure. The artistry of this top tier appears to be a celebration of the craftsmanship of the local artisans. There is an elegant carved circular archway below the pitched roof. At the top of the pitched roof is a symbol that is not a cross but looks more like the symbol used by the current day Red Cross.

My eyes and mind were occupied by all I was observing. Suddenly I was astonished as my eyes observed that on the top of the four pillars above the pitched roof was a turret in the style seen in most ancient castles or fortresses. On the side of the pitched roof were small turrets much in the style of the rook chess piece.

In observing the altar from a distance I also noted that it does not depict the crucifixion which is common for most Catholic churches. The church appears to have added a golden crucifix which they placed between the four pillars at the top. This golden crucifix feels out of place.

I sat in silence in awe of this simple structure and beautiful structure.

I wondered, what does this all mean?

I HAVE THAT FEELING

I left the chapel and walked over to the adjoining gift store. There were postcards depicting church sanctuary and the exterior of the church. There were many books about the 19th century priest Berenger Sauniere who arrived in Rennes-le-Chateau in 1885 and has been the center of controversy and mystery.

In the books and pamphlets is describes how over the next decade Father Sauniere oversaw extensive renovations to this small rural church whose roof was badly in need of repair. Also he built new buildings dedicated to Mary Magdalene. He said the new buildings were intended for a home for retired priests. There were inquiries of Father Sauniere about the source of funds he used for extensive renovation of the church and new buildings. There has been speculation that Father Sauniere had found the treasures of the Knights Templar. This has fueled mystery and speculation and brought many treasure seekers. These treasure seekers tunneled under the hill beneath the church and even dug tunnels in the building floor of the now gift shop.

I then went to building next to the church were there were artifacts and monuments describing the story of Father Sauniere showing his living conditions with photographs of him and Marie Denarnaud, his housekeeper and confidante.

I then walked the grounds of the church and adjacent cemetery before going to the restaurant Le Jardin de Marie near the church to join my friends for lunch. It was a casual outdoor restaurant with a local artist David Bailey playing the piano. He would invite people to come sit next to him and he would then play a composition as he felt the person's energy and soul. The music was amazing and brought everyone peace.

After lunch we had free time to explore the village. I immediately went back to the church while others explored the shops and other buildings. I was the only one in the church and sat in the first pew. I was drawn to this simple church and it was pulling at my heart. I did not know why. Why is there so much speculation and conspiracy?

I sat in silence. I then I asked for clarity for the intense feelings I was having siting there in the church. I decided to mediate. I sat there in silence opening my mind and heart. As I sat there in silence this overwhelming feeling of love poured over me.

What came next really surprised me. As I sat in the church in silence this story began to answer my request for clarity. A woman appeared in my vision. She was an elegant mature woman. It became clear to me that the source of what had happened in this church was due to this woman whose name was Jacqueline. She described how she had become a wealthy woman who lived in Paris most of her life. She had been drawn her entire life to the story of Mary Magdalene and decided to come to the south of France in search of the myths surrounding her. The journey in search of the myths surrounding Mary Magdalene bought her through the south of France and eventually to Rennes-le-Chateau with its rundown church. She met the local priest Father Sauniere she found in him a humble man whose love of God reminded her of her own passion. After living in the village for a while and observing this simple humble priest she decided this was the end of her search.

She arranged a meeting with Father Sauniere where she made a proposal. She would pay for the renovations of the church with a few strict conditions. Father Sauniere was grateful and agreed to her conditions.

Suddenly three of the people from my tour group came into the church and told me we were about to leave. I was disappointed as I felt there was more of the story to come. I closed my eyes and thanked Jacqueline for the gift of clarity she gave me. I caught up with the rest of our group as we walked down the street to our waiting bus. We all had wonderful experiences and wanted to return again. After dinner we all gathered, as was the custom, to share our thoughts, feelings, and observations. I shared with the group my experience inside the church and everyone wanted to hear more. I told them I also hoped I would have more visions. A group of us stayed up until midnight talking about the trip and the wonderful feelings we were experiencing in our farmhouse accommodations.

I went up to my room and quickly fell asleep. I woke up at 2 a.m. with this strong energy in my head and heart. I could not get back to sleep. After failing to fall asleep, which seemed like hours, I took out my writing tablet.

Suddenly I began to write without thinking as Jacqueline's shared her story. As I was writing I felt nothing but love. I wrote without editing as I went along. I kept writing until I noticed it was the morning twilight.

I continued writing and finished just before breakfast. I quickly showered and joined everyone for breakfast. I was amazed, I was not tired even though I had only two hours of sleep. The events of the day were full but I never got tired. That evening I went to bed again at about midnight but was awakened again with the same intense energy in my head and heart. I did not try to go back to sleep but got up and pulled out my writing tablet. I again wrote until day break. This pattern repeated again for two more days.

THE VISION

JACQUELINE ARRIVES IN RENNES-le-CHATEAU

*I*t is spring in 1886 when Jacqueline arrives in the middle of the day in a carriage drawn by two horses up the hill to Rennes-le-Chateau. All her belongs are strapped to the top of the carriage. It is time to find a place to stay for the evening. As she arrives in the village she notices the simple structure of the buildings badly in need of repair and paint. There are no buildings taller than the church at the end of the village on top of the hill. Jacqueline smiles as she thinks this is very different than Paris where she lived her entire life.

Like many European villages Rennes-le-Chateau has a complex history. The focal point of the village at the top of the hill is the Church with small shops lining the street on the ground level and homes above the shops. The church was deteriorating and badly need of repair as the roof was leaking and the interior walls were crumbling from lack of care.

In this small village curiosity has stirred the attention of the villagers as Jacqueline's coach moves into the center of the village. Jacqueline is a woman in her early sixties but you would never know it. She is beautiful, petite, slender, with stunning reddish-brown hair flowing down her back to her waist. It is not as naturally curly as it was in her youth. She walks with an elegance and presence that everyone notices. Her eyes are blue which are highlighted by her reddish-brown hair. The twinkle in her blue eyes makes you smile.

She had lived a wonder life in Paris after being rescued from an orphanage. Ever since she was a young child she had a passion for the stories and myths of Mary Magdalene. She came to the south of France to discover all the churches devoted to her. Jacqueline was drawn to this area for the reverence held for Mary Magdalene. As she rode in the countryside on the way to the village she felt her heart come alive beyond what she had ever expected.

As they travel up the street she does not notice a sign for an Inn. She has the coachman stop the carriage at the church. She gets out and is immediate greeted by the local priest Father Sauniere. Jacqueline exits the carriage and walks toward Father Sauniere and inquiries about lodging for the evening. Father Sauniere welcomes her to the village and then escorts her and the coachman to the nearby buildings where they are greeted by the innkeeper. Jacqueline thanks Father Sauniere and tells him she will see him at mass the next day.

THE VISION

JACQUELINE'S DECISION

The next morning Jacqueline arises with the sun. She is excited to go to mass this morning to see if she still has the feeling of awe, peace, and love she felt the day before. She walks down the street greeting all the villagers who are curious about this petite mature woman who has come into their village. She walks into the church and goes to the front pew. She looks up and sees holes in the roof. She notices that the walls are stained from rain water dripping down the walls due to the poor condition of the roof. The sanctuary is not inspiriting. In reality, it is giving a feeling of hopelessness. She realizes the small village does not have the funds to maintain the church.

Father Sauiere enters and stands next to the altar. He looks out over the parishioners and is surprised to see so many people. He smiles and says, "Curiosity has inspired you to be here this morning. It does not matter what brought you here but only that you are here." Jacqueline smiles for only Father Sauiere to see.

After mass Jacqueline strolls to the top of the hill to absorb the beauty of the view of the surrounding valleys and hillsides. She spends a few moments in quiet reflection. She returns to her apartment and goes to the adjacent apartment to talk to her coachman. They talk briefly and decide to go for a short horseback ride in the countryside. He returns after a few minutes with her two horses. Jacqueline has changed into her riding clothes and the two of them are off to explore the countryside.

It is later in the afternoon when they return. Jacqueline goes to her apartment and changes into a casual but stylish dress. She leaves the apartment and walks to the church. She goes inside and slowly walks to the front pew. As she walks slowly she surveys the floor, walls, décor, and ceiling of the church. She sits in the front pew again and remains there in prayer and silence. When she opens her eyes she is surprised to see many of the villagers sitting in the pews also in prayer.

Jacqueline is enjoying this simple humble village. It is much different than Paris' faster pace. The villagers are becoming more comfortable with her and engage her in conversation. They are polite enough to not ask why she is there yet you know the curiosity has captured them.

There is something very special about what Jacqueline feels here in the quiet village. She has more time to be with her thoughts and enjoy all the gifts that are there for everyone to enjoy each day. Having lived in a big house in Paris she seldom got out into the countryside to enjoy the beauty of nature and the rhythm and music of its sounds.

The next morning in church a woman about her age approaches her. She introduces herself and invites her to her home to have lunch with her and her husband. Jacqueline accepts and arrives at their farm house. Jacqueline tells them about her living in Paris her entire life and why she has come to the south of France. They tell her they are aware of the many places dedicated to Mary Magdalene in the area and will be happy to go with her to visit some of these sites.

Jacqueline notices a small creek flowing near the farm house. She excuses herself to go sit by the creek. She is loving the quietness with the sound of the running water. She notices all the life around her as the plants wave with the breezes, the bees gathering pollen, and the birds high in the sky. She smiles as she realizes this is the place she has been looking for to spend her final days. She can relax and explore the other churches and locations dedicated to Mary Magdalene.

The next morning after mass Jacqueline approaches Father Sauiere and ask to speak to him in private. They agree to meet later in the afternoon.

Jacqueline enjoys her lunch in solitude but her mind is very busy. It is the appointed time and she walks to the church to meet Father Sauiere. She walks into the church and goes to the front pew where she sits awaiting his arrival. Father Sauiere approaches her from behind the altar and sits next to her in the first pew.

Jacqueline gets a big smile on her face and then says, "Father this church is in dire need of repair." He shakes his head in agreement. Father I want to help with the repairs but first you must know about me.

THE VISION

JACQUELINE'S STORY

*J*acqueline did not hesitate as a simple smile of bliss comes upon her. Father I was orphaned at an early age. I was sent to an orphanage where I lived for many years. The sisters that ran the orphanage were kind but strict. I can remember being at the age of a blossoming young woman one Easter day as I sat at mass. The priest's sermon was about Jesus' compassion and how he saw that a young woman of the village was about to be stoned. He stepped in front of her and asked, "He who is without sin cast the first stone." The priest continued to marvel at Jesus' wisdom and compassion and how he had saved the whore Mary Magdalene.

Father his sermon upset me so. There was something inside of me that did not accept this story to be true. I began to explore my emotions that came from deep from inside me. As I listened in subsequent masses there were many more aspects of the ministry teachings that troubled me. Why were not all the Marys' depicted more as part of the life of Jesus? His love was so expansive it would be possible for him to embrace every man, woman, and child that wished to explore their own divinity. He taught others to be teachers. My struggles with the church's teachings became so strong that I knew I must leave the orphanage.

One day I walked out of the orphanage with only the clothes I was wearing. In the center of town I was afraid. I had never been outside the orphanage. As I sat near a merchant's store I saw this beautiful woman with red hair approach me. She was dressed so beautifully I thought she was royalty. As she passed me I saw how people would sneak a peek at her but quickly turn away. She walked slowly by me and looked at me with a gentle smile. After a short time she emerged from the merchants store and again smiled at me.

I was very cold the next day from sleeping outside under a tree. I walked around briefly and hunger was starting to overcome me. I again found myself drawn to the same merchant's store where I was the day before. My hunger grew and I was feeling weak. It was mid-day and my stomach was making noises. I did not know what to do.

I saw the same beautiful red haired woman walking toward me. She again smiled as she approached me. My stomach betrayed me as it made this incredible loud sound just as she passed by me. She did not say a word as she continued to walk by. She was inside the store only a short while. As she was leaving the store she was followed by three young boys carrying packages. She stopped directly in front of me and turned to one of the young boys and instructed him to give me the packages. She asked if I could carry the packages to her home. She motioned to me that it was just a few blocks away.

I took the packages and followed her with the two young boys to her home. Her home was very big and elegant. She invited me in. The young boys deposited the packages where she instructed. A mature woman then appeared. The beautiful woman asked her to prepare lunch for the two of us. As we dined I tried to not eat too quickly. When I finished my meal the mature woman again appeared with wonderful fruits and pastries. She asked about me and where I was from. I told her about losing my parents from an illness that had swept our village. The local priest brought me to the orphanage run by the church.

The beautiful woman did not ask why I left the orphanage. There was a knock on the door and the mature woman went to respond. The same two young boys returned with more boxes. She asked the mature woman to escort the boys to the guest room where she was to leave the packages. The beautiful woman then asked if I would like to stay with her. I immediately said I would. I surprised myself at how quickly I responded.

The beautiful woman then said I must follow her guidance and the rules of her home as the price for the clothing, food, and lodging. After living in an orphanage these requirements did not seem like difficult tasks.

The beautiful woman then asked me to follow her upstairs. We walked down a hallway and she open the third door. The first thing I noticed was the magnificent bed. There were beautiful decorations of many colors throughout the room and a vase with fresh flowers. On a chest sat the packages the young boys had delivered. The mature woman was standing next to something that looked like a ship's hull. The beautiful woman then turned to me and said, "First, you must bathe. You are required to bathe frequently and smell like a Goddess. Do not give others cause to wonder if you are other than a Goddess."

The mature woman assisted me to remove my clothing. She smiled and said, "They will be laundered and returned to the orphanage." After bathing I could see the mature woman had opened all the packages and placed many beautiful dresses on the bed. There were other things that I did not know what they were.

I rested the entire afternoon. The mature woman returned later and helped me dress. She told me to be downstairs after I finished dressing. As I walked downstairs I could smell incredible aromas that I did not recognize. I sat down at the table where we had lunch. In a few moments the beautiful red haired woman appeared and sat down. The mature woman then appeared with plates of food that I had never seen before. The mature woman served both of us and filled a third plate. The mature woman left the room and I looked around expecting another person to arrive, perhaps her husband. The mature woman returned and sat down. As soon as she was seated she raised her hands and we held hands as she offered a prayer. The three of us began to dine.

The beautiful woman turned to me and said, "I am Josephine and this is Marie. What is your name?" I responded that my name was Jacqueline. The beautiful woman then asked, "Can you read and write?" I bowed my head in shame and responded, "No". Josephine turned to me and said, "Never again bow your head in shame. Your education begins in the morning."

Josephine and Marie taught me to read, write, history, art, and politics. She taught me about life and people. We had wonderful adventures and visited many places I did not know existed. It did not take me long to realize that Josephine held the favor of a few select men. These were men of power and wealth.

I guess you are not surprised and realized I followed in her footsteps. Father Sauniere smiled in acknowledgement.

I have had a wonderful life. However, as time went by I could not resolve the conflict with the church's teachings. My wealth grew and I was financially secure when my company was no longer desired. I decided to follow my heart and search for the basis of the stories and myths in the south of France about Mary Magdalene. My journey on this quest have taken me to some wonderful places where Mary Magdalene is honored.

Jacqueline looked at Father Sauniere and said, "You now my story. Now, this is why I asked you here today."

THE VISION

THE CONDITIONS

Jacqueline pauses for a moment as tears begin to fill her eyes. I had heard of this simple but wonderful church on top of a hill overlooking beautiful valleys and hillsides. When I arrived I found a priest (you) of simple means with a church long neglected. As I sat in the sanctuary the very first time tears began to overwhelm me. The tears were of joy. My heart filled with joy. I could feel the love of Mary Magdalene. It was very familiar.

I then realized I was to help you rebuild the church in their honor. You may ask, in their honor? Yes, the renovated church is to honor Mary Magdalene, Mary, and Joseph.

Father Sauniere looked confused.

I will provide you will all the funds necessary to rebuild the church with these conditions.

First, the renovations shall be as I guide you. Do not worry, the renovations will be in the traditions of the church.

Second, you must not tell anyone where you received the funds.

Third, you cannot ask me any questions about my instruction or the purposes of what is to be done.

Father Sauniere agreed to her terms. She then gave Father Sauniere a sealed letter. She instructed him to take it to Paris to the person at the address. There he will receive the funds need for the renovations.

Upon Father Sauniere return the planning for the renovation soon began. Jacqueline could see the progress of the renovations each day when she came to pray. The craftsmen each day would all stop their work when she came to pray. They did so without instruction. They could feel a divinity within her.

THE VISION

THE MIRACLE

Years have passed since Jacqueline first arrived in Rennes-le-Chateau. This morning is a beautiful spring morning with a cool breeze yet the sun warms your skin. It is the type of day that fills your soul with joy and the zest for life especially in the simple way of life. The birds are signing as Jacqueline opens her eyes to their song of life. She lies in bed with her heart full of joy to the sounds and fragrant smells of spring. She gets up from bed with the difficulty that a woman who just turned 70 has getting her body to move in the morning. Her reddish brown hair, with hints of gray, flowing down her back all the way to her waist. She is petite with a slender figure. She has a youthful appearance disguising her age. She places slippers on her feet and looks out the window to a beautiful and amazing sight.

In through the window fly hundreds of butterflies that circle the room and then land on her hands, arms, shoulders, head, and everywhere in the room she looks. The butterflies are all different sizes and colors. As her eyes scan the room the butterflies take flight again and circle all around her. A few butterflies continue to perch on her hands, arms, and shoulders. Jacqueline is overwhelmed with the feeling of love showering her body.

She has a sense to close her eyes to focus and absorb the benefit of the amazing energy the butterflies have brought her as they fly all around her and the room. She closes her eyes for a few moments. She opens her eyes as a big smile spreads from ear to ear. She continues to sit there being one with the beautiful energy of the butterflies and listen to the sweet songs of the birds singing outside her window.

Jacqueline walks to the wardrobe and selects her favorite royal blue dress and wraps a yellow scarf around her neck. She sits down and slides her most comfortable shoes on her feet. The butterflies are still flying all around her. She walks out the door and up the hill on the path to the church for morning mass. The butterflies continue to fly around her as she walks along. The local villagers always enjoy greeting her each day as she always has a smile on her face and her stride is graceful and elegant. It is obvious to all that see her that she is a woman from a cultured and elegant upbringing.

Each villager is amazed to see the butterflies flying all around her as she walks along. She walks to the local bakery and turns right toward the church. The butterflies continue to surround her as she walks. There are only a few villagers inside the church awaiting morning mass.

The church renovations have been completed and dedicated by the Bishop of Carcassonne. The church sanctuary holds only about fifty people. There is simple altar with a depiction of Mary Magdalene in the base. The ceiling behind the altar is blue with many gold stars. Jacqueline walks past the other parishioners and sits in her usual place in the front pew. The butterflies land all around her creating a sea of colors throughout the church.

Father Sauniere as he leaves his residence hears the local villagers talking about all the butterflies. He walks to the church and enters the entrance at the back of the church. He stops after only a few steps and is taken back by the sea of color the butterflies have created. He looks at the walls and the ceiling as he walks to the front of the church. There are butterflies everywhere. As he reaches the front of the church he stands before the altar and turns to look out over the villagers sitting in the pews. He is stunned to see all the butterflies take flight and then return to their perches all over the church. All he sees is the magnificent colors.

Father Sauniere begins to speak but stops after only a few words. He looks down and says, "There is nothing that I can say that would match the miracle of this moment. Let us pray in silence and absorb the beauty of this moment." No one bows their head or closes their eyes. Instead their eyes are taking in all the beauty and magnificence of the moment.

A word was not spoken. The butterflies again leave their perches and began their flight all around the sanctuary. Everyone's eyes became larger as they marvel at this amazing sight. Suddenly all the butterflies fly forward and land on the altar. The mass of butterflies cover the altar in a sea of magnificent colors from every color found in nature.

Everyone sits in amazement and nobody wants to leave. Father Sauniere recognizing the miracle before them walks to the back of the church, crossed himself with holy water, and walks out into the courtyard. As he looks down the pathway leading to the church he sees all the villagers flocking to the church. They have heard of the miracle and want to see this miracle. Each person smiles at Father Sauniere as they walk into the sanctuary.

Soon every villagers is inside the church with their eyes wide open and smiling like young children about to enjoy their favorite dessert.

All of a sudden the butterflies take flight again and circle the entire sanctuary as the villagers look up in amazement. Many villagers have tears of joy flowing down their faces.

Jacqueline stands and walks to the back of the church. The butterflies continued to fly all around the sanctuary. She walks out of the church. The butterflies land and cover every space within the church. Jacqueline sees Father Sauniere standing in the courtyard. She walks up to him and asks, "Will you come see me in an hour." He acknowledged her request.

Jacqueline walks very slowly back to her apartment. She is looking everywhere as if she wants to remember every stone, pebble, flower, tree, and blade of grass as she walked. She enters her apartment and makes herself tea. She sits in her favorite chair which looks out the window. She enjoys her tea with her favorite flaky chocolate filled pastry. Her heart is full and she is peaceful.

There is a knock on the door. Jacqueline opens the door and Father Sauniere is there as promised. She can see he has a puzzled look on his face. She is not sure if his befuddled expression is related to her request for him to visit her or the morning's events at the church. They exchange their amazement at what had happened in the church. Father Sauniere tells her the butterflies are all still there. He tells Jacqueline that word of the butterflies had spread and now there were many people from surrounding farms and villages coming to see the sight. His amazement continues to bubble as he tell her that there are many people sitting on the floor as the church is filled with more people than the pews can accommodate.

Jacqueline offers him tea and pastry.

Father Sauniere takes a sip of tea and then asks Jacqueline, "Why have you asked me here?" Jacqueline responds, "My time to leave is very near. I know I told you when I first arrived here that you could not ask me any questions nor tell anyone about the source of the contributions to the church. Now that my time here is nearly over I will let you ask me one question."

THE VISION

THE SECRET REVEALED

*F*ather Sauniere paused and the said, "I have one question, why have you bestowed such a gift to me and this small church?"

Jacqueline did not hesitate as a smile of bliss came upon her.

She says, "I wanted to rebuild this church in their honor. I wanted to honor my father, mother, and wife Mary Magdalene."

Father Sauniere looks confused. Suddenly he begins to weep. He opens his eyes and kisses Jacqueline's hand.

Jacqueline looks to Father Sauniere and says, "I am ready." She closes her eyes and takes her last breath.

Printed in the United States
By Bookmasters